Written by

CANDY WORF

Drawn by

JAMES DILLINGER

GLITTERING EYE BOOKS
FIRST PUBLISHED IN THE UK IN 2021
MINEHEAD, SOMERSET, TA24
COPYRIGHT © 2021
TEXT COPYRIGHT © 2021

ISBN 9798490442066

10 9 8 7 6 5 4 3 2 1

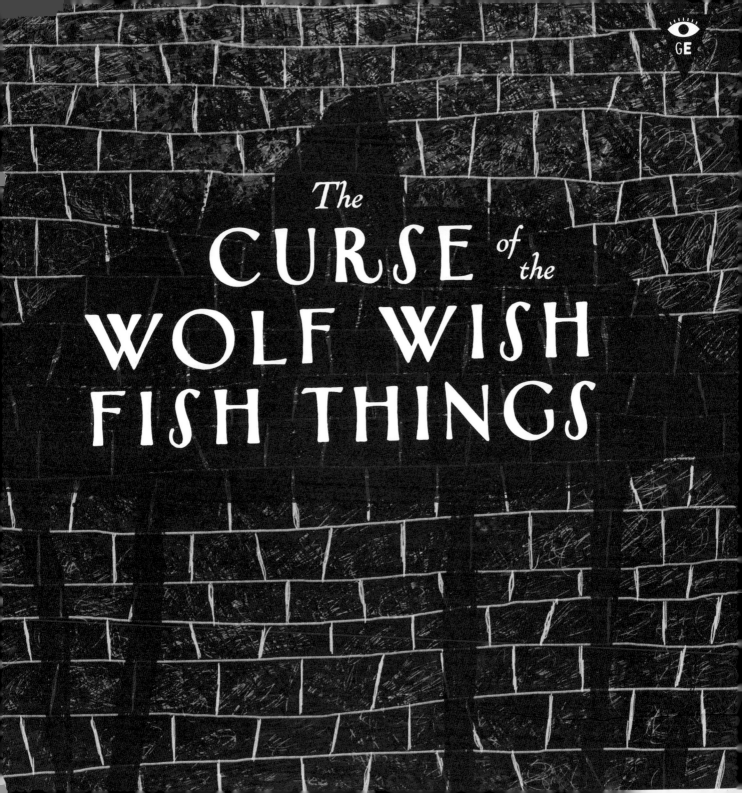

Near a ragged fishing town
as lonely as can be...
there sits an ancient wishing well,
that's older than the sea.
It harbours secret stories
that people daren't repeat...
of hollering and howling
and the dash of frightened feet.

Right down at the bottom
of that deep dark well
are the deep dark waters
where the Wolf-Fish dwell.
You can come take a look,
but don't dare make a wish!
For a wish is a wolf
that is also a fish!

If you make a wish at the well
then it will come true...
but the Wish-Fish you wake
will come after you.
There's no turning back
once the well has your wish,
hear the shrieking and the splashing
of the Half-Wolf, Half-Fish!

A wish is a fish
with a wolf's wild eyes.
It can hunt on the land
and swim through the skies!
A wish is a wolf
with crocodile skin...
Sharp dog teeth
and a killer whale fin!

They sliver from the water
and scurry up the walls,
just a flea's jump behind you...
so don't stumble or fall!
If home by midnight,
your wish will come true,
unless the dreaded Wish-Fish
catch up to you!

An explosion of thunder, lightning cracking the sky... they burst from the well like an unstoppable tide!

So flee from this place, head home for your bed!
Or a whole pack of Wolf-Fish will be happily fed!

They're
all scales and gills
and fur and spiked fangs...
And they writhe and they roar
with fierce hunger pangs.
You could try climbing trees,
but Fish-Wolves can fly...
They'd sniff you out if you hid,
so don't even try!

They will
taunt and torment you
and hunt you in packs...
And with synchronised swimming
will plan their attacks.
These Wish-Fish-Wolf-Things
are formidable foes,
swimming under the ice,
giving chase through the snow.

You will know
when they're close
from their rank and foul pong,
they're as putrid and mangy
as their barbed teeth are long.
Weighed down by the wishes
that churn in their guts,
their breath is the stench
of dead fish and wet mutts.

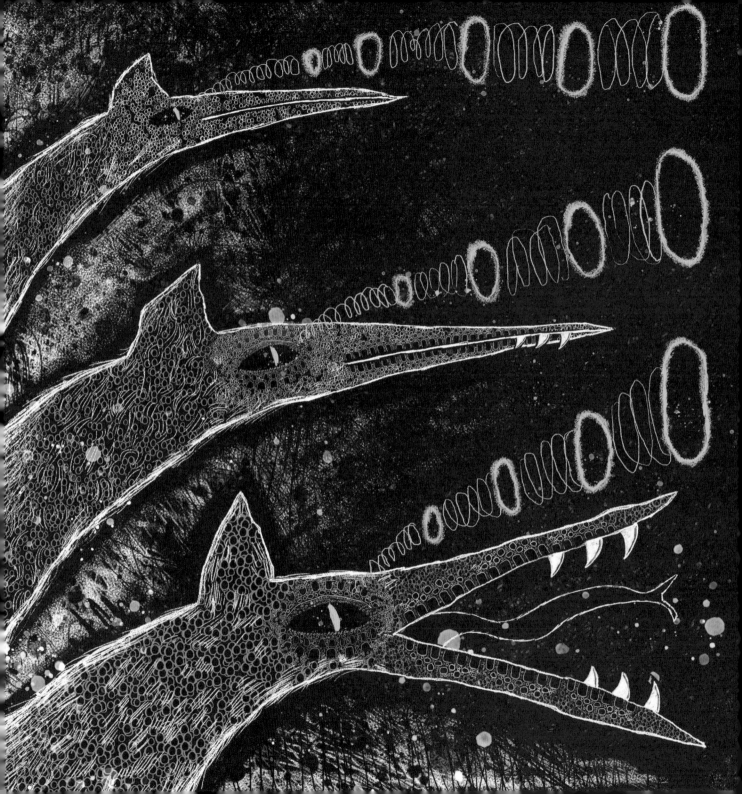

They speak only a language
of blood curdling howls,
of the scraping of talons,
ghoulish groans, grunts and growls.
No safety in shadows,
they can see in the dark.
You must outrun these wishes,
that bite, scratch and bark!

While licking their lips
and gnashing their teeth...
they feed off your fear
and they savour your grief.

They clench closed their jaws
with a fearsome fast **SNAP**!
With ravenous hunger
they fight for each scrap!

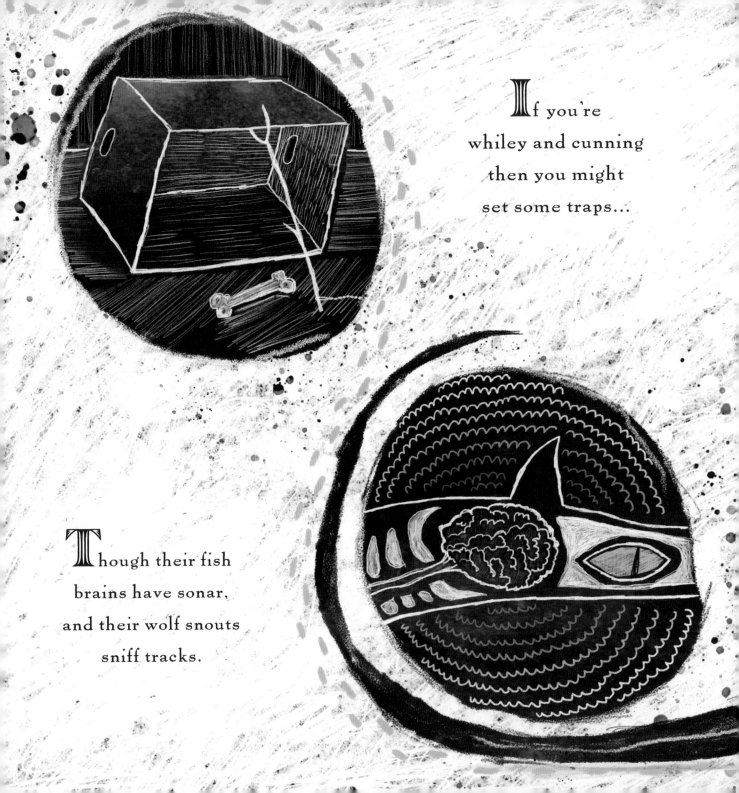

If you're whiley and cunning then you might set some traps...

Though their fish brains have sonar, and their wolf snouts sniff tracks.

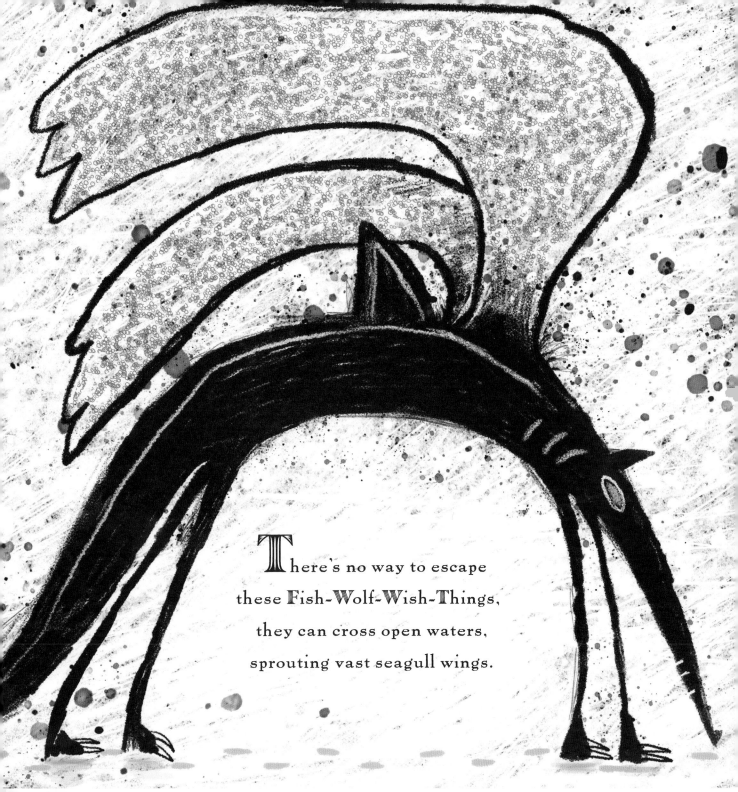

There's no way to escape
these Fish-Wolf-Wish-Things,
they can cross open waters,
sprouting vast seagull wings.

With home in your sights,
and your back to the sea...
from this terrible curse,
you could soon be set free!

If you reach your front door
from that far away well...
then the Wolf-Fish will cry...
and the ocean will swell.

An end to their hounding,
you've outrun the beasts.
Your wish will be granted...
and the Wish-Wolves won't feast.
They will fizzle into puddles,
before ceasing to be,
washing out through the gutters,
to be lost to the sea...

To the Wolf Wish fish
Things:
My dad is a fisherman,
lost at sea. I Wish
you Would bring him
back safely.
I accept my fate.

Printed in Great Britain
by Amazon